W9-CFB-934

Day at the Fair

For my brother, Mike —P. H.

To Ellen —K. M.

SIMON SPOTLIGHT
An imprint of Simon & Schuster Children's Publishing Division
1230 Avenue of the Americas
New York, New York 10020
This Simon Spotlight edition October 2015
Text and illustrations copyright © 2000 by Simon & Schuster, Inc.
The names and depictions of Raggedy Ann and Raggedy Andy are trademarks of Simon & Schuster, Inc.
All rights reserved, including the right of reproduction in whole or in part in any form.
SIMON SPOTLIGHT, READY-TO-READ, and colophon are registered trademarks of Simon & Schuster, Inc.
For information about special discounts for bulk purchases, please contact Simon & Schuster Special Sales at
1-866-506-1949 or business@simonandschuster.com
Manufactured in the United States of America 0915 LAK
2 4 6 8 10 9 7 5 3 1
Library of Congress Cataloging-in-Publication Data
Hall, Patricia, 1948-
Day at the Fair / by Patricia Hall ; illustrated by Kathryn Mitter.
p. cm. — (Classic Raggedy Ann & Andy) (Ready-to-Read)
Summary: While Marcella is at the fair, Raggedy Ann and the other dolls create a fair of their own in her
room and almost get into trouble.
[1. Dolls—Fiction. 2. Fairs—Fiction.] I. Mitter, Kathy, ill. II. Title. III. Series. IV. Series: Ready-to-Read
PZ7.H147515 Rae 2000
[E]—dc21 99-056167
ISBN 978-1-4814-5074-4 (hc)
ISBN 978-1-4814-5073-7 (pbk)
ISBN 978-1-4814-5075-1 (eBook)
RaggedyAnnBooks.com

RAGGEDY ANN & ANDY
Day at the Fair

by Patricia Hall
illustrated by Kathryn Mitter

Ready-to-Read

Simon Spotlight
New York   London   Toronto   Sydney   New Delhi

Gloucester Library
P.O. Box 2380
Gloucester, VA 23061

"I can't wait until tomorrow comes!"
Marcella told Raggedy Ann and Andy. "I'm
going to the fair! I'm sorry I can't take you.
But you might get lost."

The Raggedys didn't say a word. Everyone knows that rag dolls can't talk. At least that's what Marcella thought.

Later, after Marcella had gone to bed, Raggedy Andy sat up. "Why can't we go with Marcella?" he asked.

"Because fairs aren't for dolls, they're for people," said Raggedy Ann. "But, I'll tell you

what! Tomorrow we'll make our own fair
right here!"

Raggedy Andy was so excited, he could
hardly sleep.

The next morning Marcella kissed her dolls good-bye and hugged Fido.

"I'll be back when the clock says 'cuckoo' two times," she said. "Be good children!"

Click went the front door. Marcella and Daddy were gone.

Slam went the back door. Mama went outside to her garden.

"Finally!" said Raggedy Andy.

"Let the fair begin!" said Raggedy Ann, giggling.

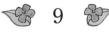

"Up I go!" cried Raggedy Ann.

"This is our very own bouncing place!" said Uncle Clem.

"Look out below!" shouted Raggedy Andy.

"Step right up! Three balls for a wooden nickel," called Raggedy Ann.

"Great shot!" said the Camel with the Wrinkled Knees.

"Uncle Clem gets a prize!" said Raggedy Andy.

"Now let's slide," said Raggedy Ann.
Uncle Clem went first.

"Whee!" he cried on the way down. "Who says fairs aren't for dolls!"

"Me next!" said Raggedy Andy.

"Be careful!" cried Raggedy Ann.

But out the window went Raggedy Andy—heading straight for Mama's tulips!

Uncle Clem reached down to help.

"Hold on," cried the Camel with the Wrinkled Knees.

But Uncle Clem went sailing toward Mama's favorite rosebush. Now there were two dolls outside!

The Camel with the Wrinkled Knees reached down to help.

"Watch out!" cried Fido. But down went the Camel. Now there were three dolls outside!

"Fido," said Raggedy Ann. "Follow me to the basement. We're on a rescue mission!"

Raggedy Ann sat down on the basement floor and thought so hard that she nearly burst three stitches in her rag-doll head.

Then she said to Fido, "Quick, out that window! You help Uncle Clem and Camel. I'll help Raggedy Andy."

"Pssst! Over here!" said Raggedy Ann to Raggedy Andy. She didn't want Mama to hear.

"I'm coming!" said Raggedy Andy. He
didn't want Mama to see.

"Grab on!" Fido said, holding his paw out to Uncle Clem.

"Hold tight!" Fido said to the Camel with the Wrinkled Knees, pulling as hard as he could.

"Way to go, Fido!" Raggedy Andy cheered.

"I knew you could do it!" said Raggedy Ann. "Now it's time to get back upstairs before Mama comes inside." Gloucester Library
P.O. Box 2380
Gloucester, VA 23061

"Hurry!" whispered Raggedy Ann.

"Fido, is that you?" called Mama from the kitchen.

"Arf!" barked Fido.

"I didn't know fairs were this exciting!" said Raggedy Andy. "But it's lucky we're rag dolls. Falling didn't hurt a bit!"

"Speak for yourself!" said Uncle Clem, laughing.

"It's time to clean ourselves up," said Raggedy Ann.

"One more knee to clean," said Uncle Clem.
"Hold still!" said Raggedy Ann.

"Good as new," said the Camel with the
Wrinkled Knees.

"Now let's clean up this room!" said
Raggedy Ann.

"Aw, gee," said the Camel with the Wrinkled
Knees. "Can't we play more at the fair?"

"No, we'd better get moving," said
Raggedy Andy when he saw the look on his
sister's face.

Before long the playroom was as good as
new. Then the dolls and Fido heard "cuckoo!
cuckoo!"

And everyone remembered—two cuckoos
meant Marcella would be home soon!

Marcella came in a few minutes later.

"I've missed you!" she said to the dolls and
Fido. "But I know you've been good. Look! I
brought surprises!"

Then Marcella told the dolls and Fido all
about her day at the fair.

"First I jumped on a bouncy trampoline," Marcella said. "Then I threw some balls and won a prize. Then I slid down a high-up slippery-slide. I was careful not to fall off."

Then Marcella stopped and looked at her dolls. "Oh," she said. "I guess you wouldn't understand. Fairs are for people, not dolls."

Raggedy Ann and Andy and Uncle Clem and the Camel with the Wrinkled Knees sat very still. None of them said a word.

Because, of course, everyone knows rag dolls can't talk!

Gloucester Library
P.O. Box 2380
Gloucester, VA 23061